ILLUSTRATED BY JAN BRETT

NOELLE

♥ *of the* ♥

NUTCRACKER

Written by Pamela Jane

Houghton Mifflin Company
Boston

To Lucy, whose childhood gave light to this tale.
— P. J.
To my niece Amy.
— J. B.

Text copyright © 1986 by Pamela Jane
Illustration copyright © 1986 by Jan Brett

www.houghtonmifflinbooks.com

Library of Congress Cataloging-in-Publication Data
Jane, Pamela.
Noelle of the nutcracker.

Summary: At Christmastime a beautiful ballerina doll who longs to dance
is discovered in a toy store and coveted by two little girls: Ilyana, who
wants to love her, and Mary Jane, who doesn't want Ilyana to get her.
[1. Dolls—Fiction. 2. Ballet dancing—Fiction. 3. Christmas—Fiction] I. Brett,
Jan, 1949–   ill. II. Title.
PZ7.J213No 1986 [Fic] 86-7254
RNF ISBN 0-395-39969-6   PAP ISBN 0-618-36922-8

Manufactured in the United States of America
RO 10 9 8 7 6 5 4

CONTENTS

Destined to Dance

t was December first, and Bugle's Toy Store was bursting with new toys and games. There were bicycles and sleds, model ships with billowing sails, and computers with puzzles to solve. There were leopards and polar bears and teddy bears, and a little pink pig. But the first thing you saw when you entered the store was Mr. Bugle's famous doll collection — "The finest in New York!" Mr. Bugle liked to boast, and it was true! There were baby dolls in frilly lace caps, gypsy dolls with bright calico skirts, and a pirate doll with a red bandana and a patch over one eye. There were dolls with pigtails, ponytails, and long curls like bed springs. The newest arrival was a ballerina doll. Her name was Noelle.

Noelle was a very unusual doll. Her knees and ankles were neatly jointed so that she could bend her legs and point her toes, like a real ballerina. She could do all five ballet positions and stand on *pointe*. Noelle was proud of that. She wore satin slippers with ribbons around her ankles and a silver and pink ballerina's dress that fluttered and floated around her like a butterfly. Her long hair was braided and twisted into a shining coil, and her skin had a faint flush, like a Christmas rose. She was a doll that any little girl would love to own, but Noelle didn't want to belong to a little girl. She had made up her mind from the moment she first bent her pretty leg that she was destined to dance!

"I have a great career ahead of me!" she said to the other dolls. "I am an artist."

"Grunt," said the pink pig. "What is an artist?"

"A great dancer!" said Noelle, and she turned a pirouette.

"Mama! Mama!" cried a baby doll. "I don't want to be an artist. I want a little girl to hold me!"

"That's because you can't twirl on your toes like I can!" sang Noelle.

The pink pig snorted loudly. "Who cares about twirling on your toes? I want to be cuddled!"

"I'd rather be scratched under my chin," purred a blue kitten, waving her fluffy tail beneath her pinafore.

"Not me! Not me!" said Noelle. "I want to dance before hundreds of people in a great ballet. That's what *I* was meant for. But first I must be discovered."

"What is 'discovered'?" asked the pirate doll.

"Like discovering a buried treasure," said Noelle, "only *I* am the treasure."

2

"I want to be discovered by a little girl," said the baby doll. "Mama! Mama!"

It was seven o'clock and beginning to grow light. The polar bear waited on all fours for children to come and climb on him, and the little pig longed to be squeezed and made to feel piggy-wiggy (which means round and pink). The blue kitten swished her long tail impatiently. Noelle stood quietly on her shelf, practicing first position. But deep down she was hoping and wondering.

Noelle was hoping she would be discovered, and wondering when it would happen.

A Bugle Call

 lyana Ingram listened drowsily to the rattle of trucks on Twenty-fifth Street. She had been having such a nice dream — something about dancing. Yes, she was dancing in a ballet, bobbing and floating like a butterfly, before hundreds of people. Oh, what a delicious feeling it was! She closed her eyes and felt the fairy wings of her dress unfold and lift her up . . . up . . .

Suddenly the living room clock began to chime. ONE! TWO! THREE! FOUR! FIVE! SIX! SEVEN! Even the chimes had a special richness this morning, as if announcing that something exciting was about to happen.

Ilyana sat up and sniffed expectantly, but no warm, buttery smell of pecan rolls or waffles wafted from the kitchen. Then it couldn't be a holiday. Besides, her red corduroy pants were folded neatly across the back of her chair, where Mrs. Ingram had put them the night before, for school.

"You'll probably be up early," she had said, smiling.

Up early! That was it! Today was December first, and Miss Taffy, Ilyana's teacher, was taking the class on a holiday outing to Bugle's Toy Store to see all the new Christmas toys!

Ilyana bounded out of bed and hurried into her pants and sweater, singing to herself.

"Bum bum be-de bum, bum bum be-de bum!"

Patricia poked her head into the room.

"Will you stop making that noise?"

"That," said Ilyana, "is a bugle call! It's a signal to hurry because today Miss Taffy is taking us to Bugle's Toy Store!"

"Oh, is that all?" Patricia yawned. "Wait until you're in fifth grade and you can see *The Nutcracker* ballet. Of course not everyone gets to go. Our class is just lucky."

It was older sisters who were lucky, Ilyana thought ruefully. Ilyana had always longed to see a real ballet. Secretly she liked to imagine that she herself was a prima ballerina — the celebrated Natasha Petrovna! Natasha's double pirouette was a flash of something winged and white; her famous flying leap — but it was Natasha's famous flying leap that had sent Heinrich, Mrs. Ingram's pet brass bullfrog, flying right out the window! He had fallen five flights and had landed in a puddle in front of the Wing Fat Sing Chinese Restaurant, denting his nose.

"I just got dizzy and lost my balance," Ilyana had mumbled, hanging her head.

"Well, you'll have to get dizzy somewhere else," Mrs. Ingram had retorted. "This apartment is too small for three people and a dizzy ballerina."

Mr. and Mrs. Ingram, Patricia, and Ilyana lived in a "railroad" apartment on West Twenty-fifth Street, in New York City. In a railroad apartment all the rooms are straight in a row, one after another, with no connecting hallways or passages. Ilyana's room was between the living room and Patricia's room. There were six rooms all together, not counting the bathroom, but none of them was very large, and all the furniture stuck out at awkward angles, which made flying leaps difficult, especially for the exuberant Natasha Petrovna.

"It's a good thing I'm so skinny," thought Ilyana, hastily pulling a comb through her hair, "but I wish my hair weren't so fly-away!" It wasn't at all ballerina-like to have fly-away hair. "If only it were thick and honey-colored like Miss Taffy's, or wavy and red like Mary Jane Igoe's." Mary Jane could twist her hair into a lovely red knot at the nape of her neck, ". . . like a real ballerina." Ilyana frowned and yanked at a stubborn tangle. Whenever she tried to twist *her* hair into a knot, it just popped right out again!

Ilyana continued her bugle song while she pulled on her boots.

"Mom, make her stop that noise," said Patricia, burying a lump of brown sugar in her oatmeal.

But Ilyana was already out the door and halfway

8

down the first flight of stairs. "Bum bum be-de bum, bum bum be-de bum!" she sang as she crunched through the snow to school.

"Children, quiet, please!" said Miss Taffy to thirty-two rambunctious second graders. She was standing on tiptoe, counting them. "Two . . . four . . . six . . ."

Miss Roe, her assistant, was frantically trying to rescue Ellie Berke's hat from several boisterous boys, who were using it as a football.

"Stay with your partners!" she panted in a shrill voice, and Miss Taffy began counting all over again. "Two . . . four . . . six . . ."

Ilyana's partner was Mary Jane Igoe. Mary Jane and Ilyana were always partners on field trips because their last names both began with *I*. Ilyana wished her last name was Brown, or Peterson, or Anastopolos — anything but Ingram — just so she wouldn't have to be partners with Mary Jane. Patricia claimed the easiest way to get a new name was to get married. Ilyana had seriously considered it, but none of the prospects looked too promising. She had always liked William FitzWilliam III, the class naturalist, but William had recently moved to Last Chance, Idaho, taking his *Periplaneta orientalis* collection with him. Tommy Kuzlowski lived right across the street, which was convenient for starting a romance, but the only thing Tommy felt romantic about was fire engines. There was always Elvin Whitechapel, of course — "Adorable

Elvin," the girls called him. But Elvin swore that he was going to live in a lighthouse when he grew up, surrounded by girl-eating sharks. Under the circumstances, Ilyana reflected, becoming Elvin's wife would probably not lead to great happiness.

But by the time the class got to Bugle's, Ilyana had forgotten all about wanting a new name.

The boys made a beeline for the machine guns and tanks.

Pop! Pop! Pop!

"Bang, you're dead!"

"Children, please stay with your partners," urged Miss Taffy. But her eyes were just as wide as theirs, and two pink spots glowed on her cheeks.

"Whooo! Whooooooo!" whistled an electric train going around and around, through tunnels and towns. High above, a stuffed monkey chattered from his perch.

"Kekekekekeke!"

Ilyana stopped to gaze at a Ukrainian doll in an embroidered pinafore.

"I have a Spanish doll with four petticoats under her skirt," said Mary Jane.

Next they looked at an Indian doll in a silk sari.

"My Indian doll has real pierced ears," said Mary Jane.

They looked at a Chinese doll and a bride doll with a wide-brimmed bonnet trimmed with ribbon and lace.

"I'm sick of dolls," Mary Jane said. "Let's look at something else."

They were turning to go when Ilyana saw her. She

was the most exquisite doll Ilyana had ever seen, a large ballerina in a fairylike net of silver and pink.

"Ohhh!" breathed Ilyana. "She looks like a flower!"

"She's a ballet doll," Mary Jane said. She was suddenly close to Ilyana, and her breath was hot against her ear. "I don't have a ballet doll. And look, she has real toe slippers." Mary Jane reached out to touch them.

"Don't touch the dolls, girls!" A saleslady appeared from behind the counter.

"I was just pricing her," said Mary Jane importantly.

"I'm afraid she's quite expensive," the saleslady said. "She costs one hundred and seventy-five dollars. She's a most unusual doll. She can do all five ballet positions and stand on her toes."

"Just the way I can!" said Mary Jane, although she was only a beginner at the Beatrice Batten School of Ballet. She had told Ilyana all about her twelve different leotards and the recital she was going to be in.

The saleslady opened a heart-shaped tag tied to the doll's wrist on which was neatly printed:

"Noelle — that's not a real name," said Mary Jane. "That's a Christmas carol."

"I think it's a beautiful name," said Ilyana softly.

"Oh, I could name her anything I want," said Mary Jane. She was watching Ilyana.

Ilyana was quiet while Mary Jane exclaimed over sleds, bicycles, and an elegant tea set with a border of primroses, all pink and gold. Ilyana discovered a Victorian dollhouse with a grand piano and a shiny brass door knocker. Mary Jane thumped it against the little red door. *Rap! Rap! Rap!*

"This," announced Mary Jane, "is definitely going on my Christmas list."

Ilyana was sure then that she had forgotten all about Noelle.

In class after lunch, Miss Taffy asked the children what they had liked best at Bugle's

"I liked the fire engines," said Tommy Kuzlowski.

"What did you like best about them?" asked Miss Taffy.

"They go *WHIRRRRRRRR!*" screeched Tommy, making a noise like a siren.

Mary Jane raised her hand.

"I liked the ballet doll," she said.

"What did you like most about the ballet doll, Mary Jane?" asked Miss Taffy.

"She costs one hundred and seventy-five dollars," said Mary Jane. A few children tittered. But Mary Jane turned and looked straight at Ilyana.

"Of course," she added, "that's no problem for me."

14

Discovery

he day after Ilyana's visit to Bugle's, a young man from the Imperial Ballet Company came into the toy store.

"I've come to pick out a doll for *The Nutcracker,*" he told Mr. Bugle with a smile. When he smiled his blue eyes got even bluer.

When Noelle heard *"The Nutcracker"* she trembled from the top of her head to her pink slippers and concentrated so hard on first position that she thought she would break.

The young man, whose name was Bruce Jennings, picked up a baby doll in a ruffled lace bonnet.

"Now *there* is a lifelike baby doll," said Mr. Bugle to Bruce.

"Yes, but a baby doll belongs with a real little girl," said Bruce, and he picked up a gypsy doll with a wide, calico skirt.

"This is a pretty doll," said Bruce, turning the gypsy

doll around slowly, "but she is not quite large enough to be seen on stage."

"Oh, on stage!" thought Noelle. "Look at me, I'm just right for the stage!"

Bruce put the gypsy doll back and picked up the pirate doll. The pirate doll glared at him with his glass eye.

"He's a fierce looking pirate," said Mr. Bugle.

"Yes, but he's not quite what I had in mind," Bruce said thoughtfully. And he put the pirate doll back on the shelf.

Then he looked straight at Noelle, standing quietly in first position.

"What control!" said Bruce admiringly. "Even our own ballerinas cannot stand so still."

"Real ballerinas cannot stand as still as I can!" thought Noelle, and a great happiness swelled in her, as Bruce lifted her gently down.

"She's unique," said Mr. Bugle. "She has real joints in her knees and ankles."

"Real joints!" sang Noelle. "I can point my toes. None of the other dolls can do that!"

"Yes, I think she will be perfect," said Bruce. "She is large and beautiful and will be seen well from the stage with the bright lights shining on her."

"Oohhh, bright lights!" thought Noelle. "I've been discovered at last!"

And Noelle was put in a box tied with string and carried away.

Noelle didn't realize that Bruce Jennings was a

prop man for the ballet. A prop man takes care of the things that the dancers will need to use in the ballet, such as toys in a ballet about Christmas, like *The Nutcracker*. In *The Nutcracker* there is always a tall Christmas tree with toys and gifts heaped around it. Bruce had come to Bugle's to buy a doll for the little girl Clara, a character in the ballet, to find under the Christmas tree. Noelle did not know she had been chosen to sit under a Christmas tree. So when she was put in a box and carried off she thought, "I will be the star of *The Nutcracker!*"

While Bruce was congratulating himself on finding the perfect doll for the ballet company, someone else was thinking of Noelle, too. Mary Jane Igoe had not forgotten the ballet doll, and she would have been very surprised to find Noelle missing from the shelf at Bugle's Toy Store where she had first seen her, standing in first position. Mary Jane hadn't the slightest idea what she would do with another doll, but there was one thing she *was* sure of: Ilyana Ingram would never have her.

That very evening, when Mr. Igoe returned from a trip to Hawaii, he brought Mary Jane a Hawaiian doll with golden skin and a wreath of silk flowers around her neck. Mary Jane hurriedly pushed the new doll into her closet with the Indian doll and the Chinese twins and begged her father to take her to Bugle's to buy the ballet doll.

"Absolutely not," said Mr. Igoe, firmly. "You'll have to wait and see what Santa brings."

"I WON'T, I WON'T!" cried Mary Jane turning pale. (Mary Jane was an expert at turning pale.) "You'll go away again like last year, and it'll be too late! I'll hold my breath!"

An ominous silence followed.

Mr. Igoe turned at the sound of a match striking behind him. His wife was lighting a cigarette. She inhaled deeply, watching him.

"What are you looking at me that way for, Nikki?" asked Mr. Igoe.

"Do you want your daughter to hate you for the rest of her life?" said Mrs. Igoe quietly. Mary Jane gave a loud sniff.

Mr. Igoe laughed nervously.

"Not much chance of that, is there, kitten?" he said to Mary Jane. "You know how Daddy likes to tease his little kitty. But deep down he doesn't mean it, even for a minute! How would you like to stroll down to Bugle's on Saturday, after your ballet lesson?"

Mary Jane nodded, and bit her lip to hide a smile.

"That doll is as good as mine," she thought.

A *Secret* Secret

 veryone in the Ingram family was busy making Christmas lists. Patricia's was neatly arranged in alphabetical order beginning with "apple blossom eau de cologne" and ending with "xylophone." Ilyana's list was much shorter. It looked like this:

Noelle
Noelle
Noelle
Noelle

"Where's the music?" teased Mr. Ingram. So Ilyana made it look like this:

"You'd better put something else on your list," said

Mrs. Ingram. "Patricia needs new glasses and I'm desperate for a new vacuum cleaner."

At school, Miss Taffy's class was planning a Christmas pageant. The theme was "The Spirit of Christmas." The children could choose what they wanted to be, and Miss Taffy would help them make up lines to recite.

"Let's try to be original," said Miss Taffy. "We now have three angels. I think three angels are enough. Can you think of something else you would like to be?"

Tommy Kuzlowski raised his hand.

"Yes, Tommy?"

"I want to be a fire engine!"

The class laughed.

"That's a nice idea," said Miss Taffy, "but I would like you to be something alive, like a wise man. We only have two wise men so far. Yes, Ilyana?"

"I want to be a ballet doll, Miss Taffy."

"All right. Now how does a ballet doll represent the spirit of Christmas?"

"A ballet doll might be given to a little girl who wants to dance and would love her," said Ilyana.

"That's a fine idea. Then Ilyana will be a ballet doll."

Mary Jane Igoe raised her hand.

"Yes, Mary Jane?"

"Miss Taffy, I don't think it's fair that Ilyana can be a ballet doll if Tommy can't be a fire engine. Fire engines aren't alive and neither are dolls."

Miss Taffy looked puzzled for a moment.

"I think you have a point, Mary Jane. Would you like to be a ballerina, Ilyana, like in *The Nutcracker?*"

"I know about *The Nutcracker*," said Ilyana. "My sister is going to see it with her class. It's about a little girl and a wooden nutcracker that turns into a prince and takes her on a magical journey."

Mary Jane raised her hand again.

"I want to be a ballerina, Miss Taffy. I'm taking lessons, and I'm going to have a recital in May."

"We have three wise men; I think we can have two ballerinas," said Miss Taffy. "But remember, your lines must convey the spirit of Christmas."

Mary Jane smiled at Ilyana.

Ilyana frowned and looked away. But she was not really angry. She had an idea, and it was going to be a secret — an absolutely *secret* secret.

After school the next day, Ilyana and Mrs. Ingram went to Fashion Avenue to buy fabric for Ilyana's costume. Snow filled the air, and a sharp wind whipped Ilyana's woolen scarf across her face as they hurried along past the bright windows of the trimming stores, looming out of the dusk like glittering ships laden with treasures — colored glass buttons and beads, ropes of silver and gold, and fine French laces the color of whipping cream. In the fabric stores Ilyana gazed wonderingly at the shelves reaching up to the ceilings, piled high with velvets, satins, silks, and chiffons. But she made her choice quickly — pale pink satin for the bodice of her costume and pink chiffon shot through with silver for the skirt. The salesman had to climb all the way up to the top of the rickety old ladder to reach *that*, but — yes — it was just what she wanted!

That evening she watched her mother gather and stitch the chiffon into a full skirt with a stiff net slip beneath to make it stand out. When the bodice was finished Mrs. Ingram pinned it to the skirt, and Ilyana tried on her new dress. Wisps of chiffon fluttered and sparkled as she twirled across the room, but the pins pricked, so she had to stop.

On Saturday morning, the day Patricia's class was going to see *The Nutcracker*, a Christmas package filled with homemade cookies and fudge arrived from Aunt Penny. Now it seemed as if the Christmas celebrations had really begun.

"I get all the jelly tots!" said Patricia, tearing off the wrappers and putting two tots into her mouth and three more in her pocket.

"No fair!" cried Ilyana.

"And I get first dibs on the gingerbread men."

"Patricia, share with your sister," said Mrs. Ingram, frowning as she struggled to turn the narrow straps on Ilyana's costume.

"Yum, fudge!" said Ilyana, biting into the dark, rich candy. "Ummm."

"Mom, she's hogging it all," said Patricia. She took

six pieces of fudge for herself and went to her room, her pockets bulging with jelly tots. She thought she would have just one piece now and hide the rest from Ilyana. But oh, how good the creamy fudge tasted! She ate two pieces, then three, then four . . . Then she settled down to read but kept thinking of crackle bars and buttercake squares, so she took three of each of those when no one was looking.

Patricia wasn't very hungry at lunch. She felt all right — just a little strange. But when it was time to get dressed for the ballet, she looked positively green.

"Are you all right?" asked Mrs. Ingram.

"Of course I'm all right. Why wouldn't I be? Stop staring, Ilyana! I just feel a little funny." And Patricia burst into tears.

"Owww! My stomach!"

"You must have the flu," said Mrs. Ingram. "You'd better go to bed."

"I don't have the flu," whimpered Patricia, "and I don't want to go to bed. I want to go to the ballet!"

Suddenly Patricia turned chalk white and ran to the bathroom.

"You can't possibly go to the ballet," said Mrs. Ingram, when Patricia was in bed with a thermometer in her mouth. "I'll call Mrs. Schumeyer and tell her you won't be coming. And don't say a word until I take that thermometer out of your mouth!"

"You don't seem to have a fever," Mrs. Ingram said to Patricia after she had spoken with her teacher. "But

27

before hundreds of people until she was blissfully dizzy. Now Noelle began to think of a little girl holding her in a different way, perhaps dancing with her, too, but because — *because she loved her*. It seemed to Noelle, while she stood in the gloom, a faraway dream of happiness.

"Once we knew children!" sighed the toys.

"I knew the sweetness of little arms!" murmured the cloth doll faintly through a cobweb.

"But how will I ever escape?" wondered Noelle. The cobwebs brushed across her, and she did not like it at all when a long millipede crawled slowly across her silver dress.

A Beautiful Secret

t was December twentieth, and the Christmas pageant was only two days away. Ilyana's costume was finished, and she had been working hard on her lines. Every night at home she sat at her desk, chewing her pencil and crossing out words, until her wastebasket overflowed with crumpled paper. Finally she was finished.

"My lines are going to be a surprise," she told Miss Taffy.

"That's fine," said Miss Taffy. She was busy helping the three angels with their lines.

"What's your ballet costume like?" Mary Jane asked her.

"It's a secret," said Ilyana.

"My mother is buying me a new costume from Dancin' Dandy," said Mary Jane, "and ballet slippers to match."

"Mine is a secret," said Ilyana.

It was a beautiful secret, too. Ilyana stood in front of the long mirror in her parents' room the night of the pageant. Mrs. Ingram had brushed her hair until it shone, and she had dabbed rouge on Ilyana's already glowing cheeks. The new dress stood out over the crinkly slip like pink and silver tissue.

"You sparkle like Jack Frost!" said Mr. Ingram.

Ilyana made a face. "Daddy, I don't look like a *boy*."

"You look like the doll you described in the ballet," said Patricia.

Ilyana wiggled her toes in her new ballet slippers and said nothing.

At school there was great excitement and confusion backstage. An angel had lost her wings and was crying pitifully, and the wise men were throwing spitballs at each other.

"*Baa! Baa!* I'm a lamb!" bleated a little figure bundled up in a fur coat. "*Baa! Baa!*"

Ilyana took off her coat and boots, adjusted her ballet slippers, and ran to the lavatory to fluff up her skirt. She hardly recognized the ballerina in the mirror, with her bright eyes and silvered skirts. Why, it was the great Natasha Petrovna making her American debut! How sublimely she twirled — faster and faster! Behind Ilyana the lavatory door opened, almost silently. It was not until she had stopped twirling and was deep in a bow that Ilyana realized someone was watching her.

"Don't you look pretty, though," said Mary Jane sweetly.

"Thank you," said Ilyana, straightening up quickly. Mary Jane was wearing a gold dress and matching slippers; her flaming hair was coiled on top of her head and crowned by a little gold tiara. But she looked strange. It was the way she was staring at Ilyana.

"You know what you remind me of?"

"What?" said Ilyana.

"That ballet doll! You look exactly like her! Of course, you wouldn't be a doll, because we aren't supposed to be dolls, are we? Which reminds me, my father is back from Japan and he's promised to speak to the Board about —"

"Oh, shut up!" said Ilyana, flushing hotly. Before she knew what she was doing, she pushed Mary Jane as hard as she could. Surprised, Mary Jane staggered backwards against the door. The color drained from her face and her eyes narrowed.

"I'm going to make you sorry for this," she muttered. She grabbed Ilyana's skirt and pulled . . . and pulled. Suddenly there was a sharp tearing sound, and part of the skirt came loose at the waist.

Just then the lavatory door opened, and Miss Taffy burst into the room.

"Oh, there you are! Ilyana, you're right after the angels, don't forget!" Then she stopped. Her eyes fell to the torn skirt.

"What's going on here?"

No one spoke. The two girls glared at each other.

Mary Jane's face was ghostly white, and Ilyana felt as if her cheeks were on fire.

"What kind of Christmas spirit is this?" said Miss Taffy. "Mary Jane, go help Ellie find her wings, and hurry! Thank goodness I have safety pins."

Miss Taffy went to work quickly while Ilyana blinked back hot tears of anger.

"I hate Mary Jane," she thought, her heart pounding. "I *hate* her! She's ruined my dress and spoiled everything!"

"What happened?" asked Miss Taffy, her mouth full of pins.

Ilyana swallowed hard. Her throat ached and tears burned her eyes, but she didn't want to cry in front of Miss Taffy, no matter what. "Mary Jane is always bragging that her father can get her anything, especially things other people want," she said in a choked voice. "I got so mad I pushed her, and then she tore my dress — *on purpose.*" Ilyana's voice cracked. Miss Taffy just frowned and went on pinning, the wrinkle in her forehead growing deeper.

"Miss Taffy doesn't like me anymore," Ilyana thought miserably. A tear trickled down her face, but she whisked it away with her tongue.

"There," said Miss Taffy finally, standing back. "At least the rip doesn't show. The angels are going on now, so hurry and remember, 'Way up high.' "

"Way up high, way up high," Ilyana said to herself over and over. "I must remember, 'Way up high.' " Backstage she could hear the angels chanting:

50

We are angels
In the starry sky.
We sing our praises . . .

They stopped. There was dead silence in the auditorium. Someone giggled backstage, and then one angel pushed another and giggled, too.

"We sing our praises . . ." one angel began uncertainly.

"Way up high!" all three finished in chorus (or almost in chorus).

Applause followed and the angels fled. Ilyana walked on stage. She was sure she'd be able to see her family in the audience, but she couldn't recognize a single face in the harsh glare of the lights. All she could think of as she stood there was how triumphant Mary Jane would be if she forgot her lines. Suddenly she realized she really *had* forgotten her lines. And no one knew them, not even Miss Taffy. She had been too careful to keep them a secret. Ilyana stood blinking helplessly into the blinding lights.

There wasn't a sound from the audience. Then suddenly a small voice piped up. "Is she a doll, Mommy?"

There was giggling backstage and a commanding, "Shhh!"

"But I *am* a doll!" thought Ilyana joyfully. And making a stiff curtsy, she began loudly and clearly:

I sit under a Christmas tree
Just as quiet as can be.

Though I cannot change my pose,
I dream of dancing on my toes.
But when I'm held by a little girl
I twirl, and twirl, and twirl . . .

And Ilyana twirled right offstage to a thunder of applause.

Miss Taffy was waiting for her in the wings with a big hug and a "Congratulations!" Beside her stood a handsome young man.

"Miss Taffy," said Mary Jane, hurrying up to her teacher, "Ilyana cheated. She wasn't supposed to be a doll. You said so, didn't you?"

But Miss Taffy, with her young man beside her, only smiled, her face flushed.

"Yes I did, but Ilyana surprised us," she said. "She was a doll who comes to life when a little girl dances with her. I think it was a nice surprise, don't you? Perhaps it would be better if you thought more about your own lines, and stopped worrying about Ilyana."

Mary Jane bit her lip and looked dangerously pale.

The young man with Miss Taffy was looking intently at Ilyana.

"You reminded me of something I'd almost forgotten," he said, smiling. When he smiled his blue eyes got even bluer.

Noël!

 t was Christmas Eve. On the steps of St. Patrick's Cathedral, carolers gathered, their voices lifted exultantly in the sharp air. Up and down Fifth Avenue people stopped to look in the lighted windows of Saks, where miniature figures in long coats and fur caps strolled down snowy, lamp-lit streets, stopping to gaze in the windows of *their* department stores. In the Great Hall, Clara and Cassandre, the French doll, danced their last *pas de deux* of the season. And at the Ingrams', Ilyana and Patricia were making popcorn balls.

"This one is for Daddy," said Patricia, putting aside a robust popcorn ball.

The sound of carolers drifted up from the street below.

"Noël! Noël! Noël! No–o–ël! Born is the King of Israel!"

"I wonder if Mary Jane Igoe will find Noelle under

her Christmas tree," said Ilyana dreamily, as the voices faded away.

"When you're my age, you'll forget all about dolls," Patricia said, licking her fingers.

"Girls, it's almost ten o'clock," Mrs. Ingram announced. "Time for bed."

"Oh, can't we stay up and wait for Daddy?" pleaded Ilyana. Mr. Ingram had disappeared into the cold night shortly after dinner.

"Go to sleep and when you wake up it'll be Christmas, and we'll all be together," replied Mrs. Ingram.

So Ilyana and Patricia went to bed. Ilyana fell asleep and dreamed she was dancing in Gingerspice Square. She broke off a morsel of scalloping from a house made entirely of Tipsy Cake (it was still warm from the oven) and was just about to pop it into her mouth when a dancer wearing a black mask and a glittering gold dress snatched it away and began to dance around her, chanting:

> *Ha! Ha! Ha!*
> *You should see*
> *What I've got*
> *Beneath my tree!*
> *All things here*
> *Belong to me!*

The masked dancer dissolved in laughter, which faded into a shrill whistle. Ilyana awoke to the familiar whistling of steam in the radiator. The first faint light was stealing into the room. Very quietly she got up and tiptoed into the living room where the Christmas tree stood, its tiny blue lights winking like stars in the boughs. Two bulging stockings hung from the bookcase (which became the chimney on Christmas Eve.) One had an *I* embroidered on it in red, and the other a *P* in green. Ilyana stood up on tiptoe and peeked in the one marked *I*. Suddenly the floor creaked behind her, and Patricia appeared in her nightgown, rubbing her eyes.

"I thought I heard you!" she whispered. "C'mon, let's take down our stockings!"

Ilyana found a chocolate Santa, a bar of strawberry soap, a new comb and brush, and a locket with a tiny rose painted on it. At the very bottom of her stocking was a small, flat envelope. Inside was a piece of paper, and on it was written:

WHOEVER DISCOVERS THIS LETTER

IS ENTITLED TO ONE YEAR OF LESSONS

AT THE BEATRICE BATTEN SCHOOL OF BALLET

Ilyana began to dance around the room, waving the paper.

"I discovered it! I discovered it!"

"Merry Christmas!" Mr. Ingram stood in the doorway in his bathrobe. Mrs. Ingram smiled sleepily behind him.

"No dancing in the living room!" she said. "Miss Batten said you can practice all you want at the school."

"I'm going to practice every single day," said Ilyana.

Patricia found a book for her under the tree, *The Story of* The Nutcracker. Mr. Ingram promised to take

her himself next year, just the two of them. On the first page was a picture of a Christmas tree hung with fruits and toys and gingerbread men, just like the one in the ballet.

Soon a sweet, buttery fragrance mixed with something spicy floated from the kitchen. Mrs. Ingram was making waffles and frying sausages. Behind the tree something glinted mysteriously. Curious, Ilyana crawled around the tree . . . and around . . . to where Noelle stood on the very tips of her pink toe slippers.

For a moment Ilyana just stared. Then she reached out, and very, very gently, as if she expected Noelle to disappear in a puff of pink smoke, she picked her up. There was something reassuring about the shining softness of her dress and her satin slippers. They were *real*.

"I can't believe it!" she said over and over.

Mrs. Ingram came from the kitchen with a wooden spoon in her hand and a dab of flour on her nose.

"Miss Taffy's fiancé certainly liked your performance in the Christmas pageant," she said.

Ilyana looked in bewilderment at her mother and then at her father and Patricia.

"He's the prop man at the ballet!" Patricia burst out. She had been keeping the secret since the night before.

"When Bruce saw you at the pageant, he remembered the doll he'd put in storage," explained Mr. Ingram, "so he resolved to ask the ballet's permission to give her to you. He wasn't sure the ballet would agree, especially in time for Christmas. Then last night,

when we had almost given up hope, he called and told me to come get her!"

"But it's just like magic," said Ilyana.

"Just like magic!" thought Noelle, tingling with happiness.

Mr. Ingram looked at Ilyana in surprise.

"Bruce told me the very same thing," he said.

Christmas night, when everyone was in bed, and New York lay glittering in the cold starlight, Ilyana tiptoed into the living room, carrying Noelle. The Christmas tree looked mysterious, its pale stars glimmering through the dusky boughs. Ilyana held Noelle close, pressing her cheek against the doll's shining hair. Noelle smelled good — new and sweet.

"Here is where I found you," Ilyana whispered, "and if I hadn't dressed up like you in the Christmas pageant, and played a doll coming to life, I wouldn't be holding you right now. Just think of that!"

But Noelle was thinking her own thoughts. Her silver dress shimmered in the starlight and her arms bent lightly, lovingly around Ilyana. They seemed to be urging her to . . . to what?

"To dance," whispered Noelle.

And *that* was the beginning of a real *pas de deux*.